BONUS BABY

ARIZONA MIRAGE

C.M. KANE

COPYRIGHT

The author acknowledges the trademarked status and trademark owners of various products referenced in this work, which have been used without permission. The publication/use of these trademarks is not authorized, associated with or sponsored by the trademark owners.

Editing & book design by Maggie Kern @ Ms.K Edits

Cover art by Cormar Creations

DEDICATION

*For everyone who has ever loved a baseball player, and everyone
a player has loved.*

PROLOGUE

Bonus Baby is the term for a young player who gets a large signing bonus when he becomes a pro.

Heath...

"Come on, baby," I said, running a hand down her back.

"Heath," she replied. "You've known this was my plan all along, so I don't know why it's a surprise. We talked about it all year, and everything is already set in motion. There's no changing it."

"Dani," I started, but she kissed me, which was always how she got me to shut up.

"You know I love you," she said as she pulled back. "But I need to not be under the thumb of someone else. Daddy keeps Mama on a tight leash, only letting her do things he wants her to. I'm not gonna let anyone tell me what I can and can't do, no matter how much I love them."

"I would never tell you what to do," I argued.

"You're trying to do that now," she countered. "You want me to give up my dream to go to college, to marry you, and go off to wherever it is you end up after the draft. That's not what I want. So, tell me how that's different from what my daddy's doing to my mama?"

I ran a hand down my face in frustration because she was right. I was trying to make her into what I wanted in a partner, not considering what she wanted.

"Promise me you'll call me," I said.

"I'm not promising anything," she replied. "I'm not gonna just go jump into a relationship when I get to Aunt Cindi's. I need to figure out who I am, though. And I can't do that while still trying to be your girlfriend. It just won't work."

"You could be my fiancé," I countered. "Then you wouldn't have to worry about anything."

"Can you hear yourself?" she asked. "You keep coming back to the idea that I should revolve my life around you. I'm not doing that. When I finish college, figure out what I wanna do, and get myself settled, maybe we can try again. I'm not promising," she added when I went to say something. "I don't want you to wait for me because we're both gonna grow so much in the next few years. We may end up finding someone who's perfect for us at that time, and I don't want you pining away for me instead of living your best life."

"You're the one I want," I said. "I don't know if there's anyone else that's perfect for me. I don't know if I can even think about being with anyone else."

"When you get to your team, you'll have other things to keep you busy," she said. "Besides, think of all the hot chicks who would love to date a professional baseball player."

"I don't care about anyone else," I said.

She looked at me, her eyes sad, then slid off the bed and got dressed.

"You need to go," she said. "Daddy doesn't like it when you're here super late, and it's already later than it should be."

The pool house was away from the main house, and we always came here to fool around. I'm sure her mom knew what we were up to, but whether her dad did or not, I couldn't say. My guess would be he didn't, because if he found out what was happening in here, there might be some strong words had.

"When are you leaving?" I asked as I sat up.

"Day after graduation," she replied. "Aunt Cindi said she wants me to get the lay of the land in town before I start school, and I'll only have about six weeks, so the sooner, the better."

I sighed because that meant I only had about a week before she was gone. That wasn't enough time, but she was as stubborn as anyone I'd ever met. When she got something in her head, there was no stopping her. God, I was gonna miss that about her.

CHAPTER ONE

ALMOST EIGHT YEARS LATER...

Dani...

"Paisley Jane Lloyd," I said, giving my daughter *the look*.

"Mama," she said, fists on her hips. "I'm old enough. I wanna have a sleepover party. It's my birthday, so I should get to do what I want to."

This child. She gave me so much joy, but the headaches she caused were on a whole other level. Stubborn wasn't even close to a good description, but she did come by it naturally. I mean, I'd been stubborn my whole life. It's what got me to where I was. Still, this was something I wasn't gonna let her get her way on.

"I know you think you're old enough," I said. "But I'm not ready for all that. It's a lot of work to do a sleepover, and some of your friends might not be ready. Would you want to hurt a friend's feelings because they couldn't stay?"

"Please," she begged, drawing the word out so long I wasn't sure when she'd finish it.

"How about we find a middle ground?" I asked. "We have your party, just like most of your other parties have gone. But you get to pick one person who you want to stay over with you. Thing is, you can't tell anyone else about the friend sleeping over because that would hurt their feelings."

"Can I have Owen stay over?" she asked.

"Sweetheart," I said. "You can have a girl stay over, not a boy."

"But I want Owen," she said, stomping her foot.

"Paisley," I said, my tone clear I was taking no more shit from her.

She gave a big, dramatic sigh, like I'd just ruined everything in her life. I had to bite my cheek to keep from laughing. It was so ridiculous.

"Fine," she said, again drawing the word out.

"You've got about a month before your party," I said. "That gives you time to figure out which friend you want to stay over. If you tell someone they get to stay over before we talk about it, you'll lose that privilege. Got it?"

"Yeah," she said with a sigh.

I'd survived the terrible twos and the three-nager age without much fuss. No one told me that a child about to turn seven would be more of an issue than those others were. It honestly scared me to think about what she'd be like as a teenager. But she was my little girl, my absolute angel, and the gift I didn't know I needed in one of the most tumultuous times of my life.

The weather was starting to warm up now that we'd hit February. Not like it was all that cold, to begin with, but still, it was nice to have a few days where wearing dresses was convenient, especially for my little girly girl. I swear, if it had ruffles, was pink, or glitter was involved, she wanted it. Dresses were her go-to, and making her wear pants when the weather was chilled was like trying to put a tutu on a gator.

"Mama," she said. "How come I don't have a daddy?"

"What?" I asked, sure I'd misheard her.

"Owen's got a daddy," she said. "Lizzy's got one, too. And Emma and Katie and Joey. But I don't have a daddy. How come?"

Oh, boy. I knew the question would come eventually, but I hadn't prepared for it to be this early. Guess I should have thought about how I was gonna answer it when I found out I was pregnant.

"How come you're asking about a daddy?" I asked her, more stalling for time than anything else.

"Ms. Kennedy said I didn't have a daddy because you're not a good girl," she said.

The tears that were threatening to fall from her eyes slayed me, but her words pissed me the fuck off.

"She did, did she?" I asked.

Paisley nodded, her lip quivering as she tried not to cry.

"Well," I said, pulling her in for a hug. "She's wrong." *And she was gonna get a lesson in some things when I spoke with her next, which would be pretty fucking soon.*

"I UNDERSTAND YOU HAVE A COMPLAINT," Michael Woods, the school principal, said when I entered his office the next day.

"That's right," I replied, sitting on the chair across the desk from him.

"You were somewhat vague in your email," he continued. "I wanted to get an idea of what the issue was before I brought Ms. Kennedy in. Is that all right?"

"Sure," I said.

"Please," he said, a hand held out. "Tell me what's going on that you need to discuss it with me."

"Ms. Kennedy told my daughter that the reason she didn't have a daddy is because I'm not a 'good girl,'" I said, using my hands to make air quotes around the last two words.

"I'm sure Paisley was mistaken," he said.

"She wasn't," I replied. "I asked her to confirm what was said more than once over a few days. I didn't want it to be true because I really liked Ms. Kennedy. But she can't be telling children that their parent isn't good, or giving reasons as to why a child doesn't have a specific parent. She has never asked me about the situation before, and I've never discussed it with her. In fact, I'm pretty sure that no one at the school knows what the situation is when it comes to my daughter and her father."

I watched him as I spoke, and the realization dawning on him was pretty clear. The teacher had fucked up, and he was trying to figure out how to get out from under whatever I had in mind when it came to recompense for the issue. What I wanted was for this, and every teacher, to not ask these types of questions. I'd thought that had gone out long ago, but apparently, there were still people who thought it was acceptable to ask invasive questions of children who may not even be aware of what was going on with them.

"My child's conception is not something that should be discussed," I continued. "There could be a multitude of things that could cause irreparable harm to both mine and my daughter's mental health, not to mention our safety, with those types of questions."

"I completely understand," he said, nodding with my

statements. "Ms. Kennedy is a relatively new teacher in our district, but she's not a first-year teacher. She should have known better than to make the statement she did, and she will be reminded of that."

"I'm thinking some extra training should be implemented as well," I said. "She should have known better, which is true. But what are the guidelines regarding this kind of thing? Has the district done training with respect to how families are not all the same? That some children might not be aware of their parentage, that they may be adopted and not know it, or that they may be a child of a traumatic experience for their mother? These are all realities of our world. And as rare as they may be, they still exist."

"You're right," he agreed. "I'm willing to request the district mandate additional training around these issues."

"Are you saying there aren't these things already in place?"

"Some are," he said. "But you've brought up some very real issues that I don't think they've taken into account. Would you mind if I made mention of this problem? I wouldn't bring up either you or Paisley, but that we had an issue where the parentage of one of our students was a concern that was brought to my attention. That the question was not only out of line but a terrible thing to say."

"I think I'd be fine with that," I said. "And if it's any concern for you, Paisley was not conceived from a traumatic event of any kind. Her father is just not in our lives and likely won't be. I know who he is and could reach out to him if I needed to, but for now, it's for the best that he is kept out of our lives."

"I understand," he said. "I wasn't going to ask, but I appreciate your volunteering the information. It's good to know that she has a strong mother who will likely help her to see what she could be when she gets to that point."

"That's something else I'd like to discuss," I said. "Kids shouldn't be pushed to declare what their future occupations will be. There is no way I would have known when I was in high school, let alone elementary school, that I would be doing what I am now. Honestly, as long as she's happy, I couldn't care less what she decided to do. She does need to learn how to navigate this world she'll grow into, but how she makes money and lives her life, are far down on my list of things I'm worried about."

"Like I said," he said. "She couldn't have asked for a better role model than you."

"Thanks," I said.

We wrapped up the meeting quickly, with a promise that my daughter's teacher would be given some extra training on why what she said was not just wrong but also potentially dangerous. With the way the world is connected and the millions of places our lives show up, if someone was hiding from someone dangerous, the things she said could have ended much differently than this.

CHAPTER TWO

Heath...

"*Arizona?*" *I'd asked my agent when he called me just before Christmas.*

"*Yeah,*" *he'd replied.* "*It's a good move, and they want you. They feel like you've got what it takes to get them to the end goal. You've been fighting an uphill battle in New York. Going to a smaller market, where your impact can be felt right from the get-go, is the right move. Who knows? Maybe it'll be just what you need to get yourself back to the top of the heap.*"

"*Yeah,*" *I'd said with a sigh.*

I'd known they'd been shopping me around, but I wasn't sure whether they'd trade me or let me play out the rest of my contract. It was smart for them to at least try to get something for me, though, and I didn't begrudge them that.

"*When do I report?*" *I'd asked.*

"*As soon as spring training starts,*" *he'd said.* "*Do you want me to work on getting you a place down there?*"

"*Yeah,*" *I'd said.* "*Not right in the middle of the town, though. I hate living in the city. I miss having space around me.*"

"I'll do my best," he'd said. "Long lease? Or do you want me to find something for you to buy?"

"Just a lease," I'd said. "I don't plan on being there after the season."

He'd found me a place in Scottsdale, where the team held their spring training. It was close enough to Phoenix and the stadium that it wouldn't hinder me when I needed to get to games during the season. I'd moved about a month before I had to report, so I'd have time to get settled in and figure out where everything was. Nothing worse than going to a new town and not knowing where the grocery store was.

I was able to get into the training facility for the team shortly after I arrived, and it was helpful to get to know some of the guys from the team before we got going. Sure, I'd known a few of them from playing against them the handful of times we did, but it's different being on the same team. They'd also told me about all the best places to go to get the best of pretty much everything in town, which was really nice.

Having spent six years in the New York area after my call-up, I'd grown to love pastries, which were definitely not on the diet plan, but were a good treat occasionally. The thing was, I wanted good pastries, not just average. I wanted what I remember from back home, from what Mama would make for the holidays and what *Nonni* would make for special occasions.

Even when I wasn't playing, when the team was on breaks, getting home was rough. Early on, I couldn't even afford to go home unless someone paid for the tickets. I'd always thought I'd be rolling in it once I signed the contract, but that was so far from the truth it was sad. The minor leagues were fun, for sure, but not having any money wasn't easy when I was on my own. Before I got drafted, my parents paid for everything. Once I was on my own, though, I realized exactly how expensive the world was.

It wasn't until I got my bonus when I was called up that I started to be able to afford the luxuries I'd always dreamed of. Hell, I'd barely had enough to get by. Thankfully, a few of us wanted to room together, so we saved and could at least live. That bonus I got when I got the call-up for the first time was amazing. Much as I wanted to do all the things I'd thought about, I was smart and put most of it away to save. After having six seasons of the larger contract payments, I'd been able to buy my parents a house so they could have the retirement they'd always wanted.

My plans for the future were still in flux, mostly because I wasn't sure what it held. I thought I knew what I wanted, but that didn't work out. I wanted a family, but none of the women I'd met or gone out with worked out. They just weren't right for me. Either that or I was still stuck on the one who got away.

CHAPTER THREE

Dani...

"Thanks for watching her," I said. "Since I'm taking Saturday off, I need to get everything done at the shop early. At least there aren't any weddings in March. The first one isn't until the third week of April."

"She's always welcome to stay over," Aunt Cindi said. "We have a great time together, don't we, Bug?"

"We do," Paisley said. "Can we do pictures again?"

"Why don't we figure out dinner first?" I asked.

"I've got spaghetti sauce going," my aunt said. "Paisley and I can make the salad if you want to put the garlic bread in the oven."

"Sure," I said.

We got to work making dinner and then sat and ate. My aunt had been a godsend when I first moved out here. After we found out I was pregnant, she helped me figure out the logistics for everything. She kept Mama and Daddy away, letting them know I'd caught the flu over Christmas that first year, and once Paisley was here, she kept them away. Of course, they finally came out, demanding answers, and that was a shit show of the most epic kind. It was all we could do to keep them from hauling us back to Texas with them.

Becoming a mother was the best and most challenging thing I'd ever done, but I believe Paisley saved me from becoming the second generation of what my mama was. She married Daddy when they were just out of high school. When Jacob was born, Mama was stuck. At least she only had my older brother and me, though. I'll never know how she kept from getting pregnant after me, but I'm glad she didn't.

I didn't want to just be a mom. I loved it, but I was more than just a one-dimensional being. I had hopes and dreams and aspirations. Paisley had thrown a wrench into some of my plans, but the last few years had been amazing.

"What kinda cake are you making for me, Mama?" Paisley asked around a mouthful of spaghetti.

"Please don't talk with food in your mouth, baby," I said. I swear, manners aren't easy on kids.

"Okay," she said after she swallowed, then proceeded to shove another forkful in.

"We've tried every kind of cake I can think of," I replied. "And every single time, you've gone back to chocolate. Did you want to try a new kind for this birthday or do you want a different flavor?"

"No," she said, drawing the word out. "What are you putting *on* the cake? The decorations part."

"Oh," I said, realizing what she was actually asking. "What did you want?"

"Barbie, duh," she said, and I had to laugh.

"And what colors?"

"Uh, pink, obviously," she said.

The sass that had crept into her voice reminded me that

we needed to have a conversation about respect again, but that could wait for another day. We finished dinner, and I headed back to my place just two doors down. I'd lived with my aunt when I first moved and for the first two years of Paisley's life, but when I started working for the bakery and started moving up, I felt ready to be on my own.

Aunt Cindi owned a couple of houses along the same street that she rented out, so we decided to try it that way to begin with, and it worked out well. After a few years, we worked out a lease-to-own contract, so I was on my way to owning the home my little girl and I shared. It made the issue of childcare work out for weekends and the occasional days when I had to be in extra early.

Now that Paisley was in school, things were even easier. The rare times I needed someone to watch her overnight and get her to school were few and far between, mostly around when the bakery was overly busy or I needed to get extra work done to have a day off. Margie, the bakery owner, was helping me gain experience of the management side of things, too. She'd wanted her daughter to take it over, but Savannah hated the shop. She kinda hated her mom, too, but that was a whole other situation that I avoided at all costs.

By the time I climbed into my bed, I was definitely ready to sleep, which was good, because three in the morning would be here entirely too soon.

"You know you could've just taken the day," Margie said when she walked in on me finishing my daughter's cake. "It's not that much that we need you here."

"I know," I replied as I tucked the cake into its box. "But

I always feel bad when I take a day and don't get everything set up beforehand."

"I've been running this place since I took it over from my mama," she said. "Been working here since I was big enough to push the buttons on the machines, too. It's not a big deal for me to do it all. Besides, that little Paisley girl is getting so big, you need to spend time with her before it slips away."

The way she said the last bit, with a little bit of a scratch in her voice, tore me up. I didn't want my relationship with my daughter to end up the way my boss's did or the way my relationship with my own mother had. We still talked, but she never forgave me for keeping Paisley away from her. She said I stole her chance at being a grandmother because she wasn't there right from the jump.

"Believe me," I said, pushing all the emotions away. "Paisley and I are doing just fine. We spend a lot of time together, just the two of us. I know what she likes and doesn't, and I make sure that I let her explore whatever she wants to know about."

"Yeah," she said with a sigh. "I should've been a little more like that with Vannah. But that's not something I can fix now, so I guess I'll just let it be."

I didn't know what to say to that or if it even needed an answer, so I kind of just got started on the next project for the shop, which was the tiny tarts and flakey Danishes. It had taken me some time to be able to make them as good as Margie, but once I got it down, she handed the whole process over to me.

What I loved most about making them was that they were simple but complicated, and it was always fun when they came out just perfect. Once I had the dough formed and ready to go, it was pushing toward the time the shop was set to open.

"Would you mind?" Margie asked, then continued when I looked at her, confused. "I'm just not really up for dealing with the public yet. Kim was supposed to be here, but she called and left a message saying that her son was throwing up all night. She didn't want to chance her bringing in some bug to share with the world."

"I gotta say, I'm thankful for that," I said. "Last thing I need is catching some stomach bug and taking it with me to the party tomorrow."

"Once it gets a bit later, I'll call Teri," she said.

We had a handful of employees we could call in when someone didn't show up, but some were more reliable and available, so we tried to ensure we shared the opportunities when we could. Like me, Teri was a single mom, so she had to wait until her kids were in school before she could come in. I knew how fortunate I was to have an almost live-in childcare person living next door.

"I got you," I said and headed out to the front of the shop to open it up.

The display cases were already loaded with the first round of pastries, so I only had to make sure the register had change in it before unlocking the door and turning on the "open" light.

"Good morning, Mrs. Rodgers," I said as the sweet older woman came through.

"Aren't you a sight for sore eyes?" she replied.

"Do you want your usual?" I asked.

"Does that make me stuck in a rut?" she asked.

"Not at all," I replied with a smile. "It just means you know what you like. Nothing wrong with that. I usually eat the same thing each morning myself."

I walked behind the counter and pulled out a kruller before pouring a small black coffee for the regular customer. Her bright smile when she approached the counter showed she was in especially good spirits today.

"I'm gonna get a few of those amaretto cherry donut holes, too," she said.

"Oh, really?" I asked. "Feeling a little festive today?"

She leaned in, like she was gonna share some secret conspiracy, and said, "There's a man at the home who was flirting with me last weekend. I think I'll see if I can entice him to come back to my place after breakfast."

The scandalous way she said it and the fact that her cheeks blushed through the powder on her cheeks told me she was smitten.

"Make sure you're safe," I said.

"At my age?" she asked, incredulous.

"Diseases are running rampant through your age group," I said. "I don't want you to end up sick if you can use a little bit of precaution."

Her cheeks grew even redder, and she covered her mouth when she giggled.

"I never even thought of that," she finally said when she'd composed herself. "I thought you were worried I'd end up pregnant or something."

"Miracles still happen," I said as I set the small box with the donuts on the counter.

She paid, gathered her things, and headed out. I just had to laugh because I couldn't imagine what my life would be like when I got to her age.

CHAPTER FOUR

Heath...

It was earlier than the ass crack of dawn, but it was the second week of games, and every damn one of them started at one. That meant I had to get to the stadium well before I liked to even roll out of bed. But that was the way the spring went. They were all early games, and us regulars played a couple three innings at most. It was more the practice of working together. We got a month of this, then it was time for the real deal.

I'd tried all the chain coffee shops, but they only had cardboard-tasting pastries. I wanted something fresh that wasn't mass-produced and actually tasted like real food—the butter, the sugar, the flavor. All the things I limited myself with but would never cut out completely. Moderation was the key, and I'd learned how to be moderate when it came to sweets and things that were strictly off the menu.

Several returning players had recommended the little shop near the stadium, saying they did a great job on their desserts for events and such. Not like it was the official bakery for the team or even for the players, but it was definitely one they recommended when asked. I'd checked the website and saw they were open early, so I decided to give them a try before I headed to the stadium to get things going.

Opening the door, a little old lady was coming out, so I held it for her.

"Well," she said, her smile mischievous. "If I were about fifty years younger..."

She let the sentence trail off, not finishing her thought. I knew what she was thinking, though. I'd have to be an idiot not to get the innuendo. Instead of confirming or denying what she was thinking or how it made me feel because the thought of it, even peripherally, wasn't something I wanted in my brain, I just smiled and walked in.

"Welcome in," the woman behind the counter said without looking at me.

I wandered toward the glass case with pastries in it and began to check them out. Not willing to just settle for anything, I wanted to see what they had before I made my decision. Absolutely everything in the case looked delicious. Nothing too big as to overdo my restrictions, but they were definitely enough to get more than a little taste of each. This might have been a mistake to come here because I was likely going to be getting much more than I'd originally planned. It wasn't like I couldn't take them home with me, though, so I figured I'd get a few to sample.

"Can I help you find something specific?" the woman asked.

When I looked up, it was like I'd been punched in the gut. There was no mistaking who she was, even though almost a decade had passed. She was just as beautiful, if not more so, and I had to suck in a breath to remind my lungs how to breathe. She hadn't really looked at me when she'd come over because she raised her head and gasped when her eyes landed on mine.

"What are you doing here?" I asked, just as she asked the same thing.

I laughed because what the fuck else could I do? The thought of seeing her again, even in some random place, hadn't been on my radar in what seemed like forever.

"Why are you in Arizona?" she asked.

"I was traded here," I said. "But what are you doing here? I mean, I know you came to go to school, but I haven't heard from you since you left. Honestly, no one I've talked to back home knew what was going on with you. How are you?"

Her eyes were wide because clearly, she hadn't expected to see me. But there was something else in them I couldn't quite put my finger on.

"You can't be here," she said. "This isn't right. You're supposed to be in New York."

"Hey, baby," I said, reaching a hand out toward her. She pulled back like she was afraid of me or that touching me would somehow make it real that I was here. "What happened to you?"

The question was rude, but I needed to know. After I'd been drafted, everything happened so fast that I never got a chance to check in on her. When I went to contact her once I'd settled in Florida with the rookie team, the number didn't go through. It said it'd been disconnected, which made me both mad and worried. When my parents tried to get in touch with hers, they refused to talk to them. None of our mutual friends knew anything, either. She'd basically ghosted the entirety of our town.

"I can't talk to you right now," she said, still backing away.

"Dani, please," I said, following her movements on the other side of the case.

"No," she said when she reached the end of the cases next to a doorway to the back of the shop. "No, you need to stay away. You can't come near me."

She ducked between the swinging doors, ones like they had on the saloons on the old western shows my dad watched, and disappeared from sight. I stood there, utterly baffled at what had just happened.

CHAPTER FIVE

Dani...

"Hey," Margie said when I burst into the kitchen. "Everything okay?"

"No," I said, and heard my voice pitching up. "No, nothing is. I need to go."

I didn't wait for an answer. I just pulled my apron off and hung it on the hook by the back door, grabbed my purse, and crashed out the back to the parking lot. By the time I pulled into my driveway, I realized I hadn't been paying attention and had driven home on autopilot.

Why was Heath in my bakery? Why was he even in Arizona? I mean, he said he'd been traded, but how had I not known that? What was I going to do? I shut the door, and I slid to the ground, my whole body shaking and my brain going a mile a minute.

No. No, no, no. This isn't supposed to happen. This can't be happening.

The thoughts just kept pummeling me over and over again. I had to keep him away because if he ever found out...

I stopped my brain because it wasn't productive. What I needed to do was talk to my aunt. She'd been more than just my support system. She was my absolute rock. Navigating the medical and insurance side of things was terrifying for me, but we figured it out. Now, though, I needed her again. This time, to keep Heath at bay and to protect Paisley's privacy. Her safety was the most important thing.

It wasn't that I thought Heath would be a danger to her, just that she couldn't be thrust into the limelight that surrounded her father. Much as I loved Heath when we were young, I knew that I didn't want to live my life in a fishbowl. It wasn't fair, and it wasn't something I would be willing to subject my daughter to. The number of celebrity kids who ended up messed up because of the notoriety was staggering, and I wouldn't let it happen to my little girl.

The reason I deleted all social media, changed my phone number, and left Texas without ever planning to go back was to make sure I didn't live like that. It was why my parents had been kept out of my life since I moved. They were the kind of people who put everything in their lives online, and I mean *everything*. If they wanted to expose themselves, that was their decision, but I was done being a piece of their pretend life.

My brother had followed suit shortly after I left. He saw how they spiraled and tried to use him to get to me, tried to use him for their own selfish shit, and didn't understand that not everyone wants to be the center of attention. When he called my aunt to talk to me, I laid it all out for him. It was before I knew I was pregnant, but it didn't change anything. I was still going to be distancing myself from them.

It had taken him a bit more time to disengage, but once he did, we actually got close. Now, we talked regularly via video, and he even came to see us after he got married. When my nephew was born, he saw the wisdom of what I'd done and thanked me for helping him to see what was going on. Neither of us talks to our parents, and from what I've heard, they are just miserable. It's their own fault, though. I tried to tell them it wasn't right, tried to step back, stay out of their pictures, but they pushed me because I was their child, and they could make me do whatever they wanted. It wasn't illegal to post pictures of me online, so they were gonna do it.

Pulling my phone out, I called my aunt. She'd know what to do. If she didn't, she'd know who to send me to.

CHAPTER SIX

H eath...

What the fuck just happened?

The question rambled through my brain, and I couldn't quite figure out how to even begin to find the answers to that question.

"Oh, sorry," an older woman said as she entered through the doors Dani had just slammed through. "I didn't realize you were out here. How can I help you?"

"I need to speak to Dani," I said. "It's urgent."

"What is this about?" the woman asked, and there was a heavy dose of disdain sprinkled on those few words.

"We're old friends," I tried, hoping it would be enough to get me the information I needed.

"Yeah," the woman said, clearly unimpressed. "I can take your name and number, but that's the best I can do."

Dammit. I scrubbed my hand down my face because, one, it was entirely too fucking early for this shit, and two, I needed to find her.

"My number hasn't changed since high school," I said.

"She knows the number. I need to talk to her because there is something wrong, and I need to help her fix it."

"I'm afraid I can't be of more help," she said. "Was there something you wanted to purchase?"

I didn't need a fucking donut. I needed to find Dani. Instead of taking my frustration out on the woman behind the counter, I just turned and walked out. I was glad that Dani had people around her to help, but she didn't need to be protected from me. She was everything to me, and she just disappeared. No, this was a case of finding bigger guns to aim at this problem.

As soon as my car started, I connected my phone and called my agent. He was the only one I could call with this kind of question. It needed to be handled discretely, but it also needed to be handled now.

"Morning," Duncan said.

"I need a favor," I replied. "It's personal, not related to baseball, and it has to be done on the down low. Like, I need no one to find out about it. At all."

"You in trouble?" he asked, and I heard the worry in his voice.

"I don't think so," I said. "I just ran into someone from my hometown. There are some questions I need answered, and I'm not sure how to go about finding her to get them. Whatever this is, it needs to stay away from the press completely. It needs to stay between you and me and no one else."

"This sounds serious," he said.

"As a fucking heart attack," I replied.

"Okay, shoot," he said.

"Shit," I said. "I don't even know where to start."

"How about a name," he suggested.

"Dani," I said. "No, her first name is Danielle. Danielle

Lloyd. She came to Arizona for college but ghosted the entire town once she landed. None of my old friends from high school have talked to her or even heard anything about her since she left."

"Old girlfriend?" he asked.

"Should have been fiancée," I replied. "She didn't want to travel all over or be owned by me, which wasn't what I wanted anyway. Her mom kind of ended up stuck with her dad because she got pregnant. Dani was determined to get her career going before even thinking about marriage."

"You don't happen to know her birthday, do you?"

"It's the day after mine," I said. "She always teased me on my birthday, saying she was hanging out with an older man. We were less than twenty-four hours apart in age."

"Okay," he said. "What information do you want? How deep of a dive do you want me to do?"

"I don't want her to know I'm looking into her," I said. "I ran into her here in Scottsdale, so she's local to me."

"She's not still in Texas?" he asked.

"Unless she's got a twin, which she definitely doesn't, then no," I said. "She freaked out when she saw me. I don't know what, but something is going on with her. If she catches wind of you searching for her, she might run. I don't want to lose her again."

"Again?"

"Yeah," I said. "I lost her when she left for college and she disappeared. Her parents never liked me, so I figured they were the ones who made it happen. Talking to friends who are still in town makes me think she left absolutely everything behind and started over here. They said her parents kind of went off the deep end, telling people she died and shit. The only thing I don't know is why."

"Got it," he said. "I've got a guy who can do some

simple searches that shouldn't draw too much attention. I'll make sure he knows it can't be obvious."

"Don't mention my name," I said. "If she realizes someone's looking for her, that's one thing. If she realizes it's me, it's game over."

"I understand," he said, but it sounded like a platitude. "I'll let you know what we find."

"Not by text or email," I said. "Just send me something that says you've got information. I'll come see you and get the details."

"Okay," he said, and this time, I felt like he actually got what I was talking about.

I disconnected the call, climbed out of my car, and walked into the stadium. Until I got information, my brain was gonna be split, and there wasn't a damn thing I could do about it.

CHAPTER SEVEN

Dani...

"And you're sure it was him?" Aunt Cindi asked.

"I am," I said.

We were sitting at her kitchen table. She'd been working from home and told me to come right over.

"Does he know about Paisley?" she asked.

"I don't know," I said, still flustered by the sight of him. "He didn't say anything about her, but I didn't really give him a chance to say much of anything."

"So," she said with a sigh. "What's your plan?"

"I don't know," I said. "I just know he can't find out about her. It wouldn't be fair to her or him. He would want to be in her life, and that would just confuse her. If the press found out? Or his parents?"

"They're not as bad as yours," she said.

"I don't know," I said. "I haven't even thought about them, to be honest. They'd surely wanna get to know her. I can't imagine that going well, either."

"Maybe you should talk to him," she said. "Not about

Paisley, but to see what he wants, what he knows, and what he's looking for."

"I'm terrified I'll slip up and say something," I said. "But he's got money, so if he wants to find something out, he might not give me a choice."

"You said he's playing for Arizona?" she asked, pulling out her phone.

"He said he was traded to Arizona," I said. "I don't know anything about the teams, so I have no idea what that means. Last I saw, he was still playing for New York."

"Let's let the search engine make its money," she said, tapping on her phone. "Yup," she said after a minute. "Looks like he was traded around Christmas. He's sure grown up."

I'd noticed that, too. I mean, amid the panic, it was clear that he was a top-level athlete, kept in shape, and hadn't skipped any of his training. God, it was like being fifteen again, the way my stomach did a little flutter at the thought of him. Of course, things lower fluttered, too, but not in the same innocent way as they had way back when.

"There's a game today," she said. "It starts just after one. I'll buy a ticket. You go to the game and talk to him. Paisley can help me get things ready for her party. I'll tell her you're working on her cake. Which, by the way, didn't come home with you, did it?"

"I'm lucky I remembered to grab my purse," I said. "What do I tell him?"

"Tell him the truth," she said and stuck her hand up when I went to argue. "Not about our girl, but about why you left home, why this move was so important to you. Feel him out. Tell him you panicked when you saw him because you thought he was gonna tell your folks."

"I think I can do that," I said, nodding. "Okay, yeah, I think that will work."

"Don't stress," she said.

"Easy for you to say," I replied.

"I'm serious," she said, looking me in the eye. "You are an amazing mom and a great person. There's nothing to be afraid of. If you feel like he might be decent, then you go from there. Don't dump everything on him, but don't shut him down, either. Just talk to him."

I took a shuddering breath, then nodded.

"That's my girl," she said with a big smile. "I put your phone number in for the ticket to be sent to you in a text."

Just as she finished the words, my phone pinged.

"You've got this," she said. "I promise. You'll be fine, and so will Paisley."

"I hope you're right," I replied, getting up.

One thing I wasn't gonna do was go to this game looking like I'd just crawled out from under a rock. If I was gonna see Heath, I might as well look like a million bucks.

"Thank you," I said, giving my aunt a hug. "You really are the best person I know."

"I don't know about that," she said. "But I do my best."

CHAPTER EIGHT

Heath...

I'd played like shit, which normally wouldn't bother me, but this thing with Dani sort of knocked me for a loop. Not the seeing her as much as her reaction to me. I didn't know what had happened since we split, but it couldn't have been good.

"Hey, Tennyson," someone shouted.

I looked up and saw the ball boy waving me over.

"She said she knew you," he said.

I turned and saw Dani standing there, and just like last time, my breath caught. If I'd thought she looked beautiful at the bakery, it was nothing compared to seeing her here, under the sunshine in the stands. It took me back a decade or more to the first time I'd seen her.

"Thanks," I said offhandedly to the kid, never taking my eyes off her.

"Hi," she said.

"Hi," I replied.

"Umm..."

"Come on," I said, holding a hand out.

The game continued, but I'd been done for an inning, so I helped her down into the dugout. Catcalls came from my teammates, but I ignored them, guiding her through the guys and down the tunnel toward the clubhouse.

"You sure this is okay?" she asked. "I mean, aren't there going to be guys showering or something?"

"We'll be fine," I said. As we got closer to the locker room, I steered us off to the side to a treatment room, closing the door behind me. "Hey," I said once she'd turned around.

"I'm sorry," she said, and I looked at her. "For the way I reacted this morning. It wasn't so much you, just the reminder of back home."

"Okay," I replied.

As she stood there, I looked at her, marveled by how great she looked. I wanted to pull her into my arms and lose myself in her again, but she was a different person now. We both were.

"My parents weren't as nice as you thought," she said. "They tried to pressure me to stay in Cloverleaf, to find a guy to settle down with."

"But not me," I said.

"No," she said with a laugh. "No, you were definitely not the person they wanted me to settle down with. Do you remember that guy, Richard Barton?"

"You mean Dickey?" I asked.

"Yeah," she said, shaking her head. "That's who they wanted me to be with. Hell, they invited him to dinner more times than I could count. It's why you never got to have dinner with us."

"I never knew that," I said.

"Even after I told them it wasn't gonna happen, they kept inviting him," she replied. "Of course, he was too dumb to realize that I didn't want to be with him. God, my parents basically tried to sell me off to his family. It was really weird the last few weeks. It's why I came out here. I had to get away, and thankfully, my aunt knew what was what. The promises I made to my parents, and all the lies I told them. It had to be done, though."

"I'm glad you got out," I said, not knowing what else to say.

"Thanks," she said.

"I would have taken you with me," I said, although I had no idea how that would've worked. "Why didn't you tell me?"

"You didn't need the distraction," she said. "I didn't want to pressure you into a life you weren't ready for."

"All I ever wanted was you," I said.

"No," she said. "You wanted baseball more than me."

"I'd give up baseball for you," I said.

"I would never make you make that choice," she said. "That kind of ultimatum never ends well for anyone."

She had a point, so I nodded. Still, I would go to the ends of the world for her. She had to have known that back then.

"Even if you did," she continued after the long pause. "I still wouldn't have gone with you. I needed to find myself and figure out what I wanted in life. Until that happened, I would've been just your girlfriend, fiancée, wife, or whatever. At no point would I have been myself, because I didn't know who I was."

"Do you know that now?" I asked.

"For the most part," she said.

"Does that mean we could try again?" I asked, praying her answer would be yes.

"Heath," she said as she stepped closer to me. "My life is

here. I'm not gonna be traipsing all over the country with you as you play. I can't do that. I have responsibilities now, a life that is important to me. I'm not going to throw away the last however many years just because you showed up. That's not who I am anymore."

Scrubbing a hand down my face, I nodded. It wasn't fair to pop back up in her life after all this time and expect her to drop everything to pick up right where we left off. Still, I wasn't gonna let her go without at least seeing if something might still be there.

"Would you go to dinner with me?" I asked. "Just as old friends, of course. Maybe take me to your favorite restaurant?"

It was almost like begging, but I didn't care. From the moment I left her to the moment I saw her again, she had been the one I always wanted.

"This isn't the best week for this," she said but wouldn't look at me.

"Next week is fine," I said. "Anytime is fine. I really want to catch up."

Her phone started ringing, and she pulled it out, her face dropping.

"Shit," she said, answering the call. "Hey. Can I call you in five minutes?"

I couldn't hear whoever was on the other end of the call, but her eyes were bright, so whoever it was, they were important to her.

"Okay," she said. "I'll call you back." There was a pause, and then she said, "Love you, too."

Those words caused an ache in the middle of my chest because she used to say the same thing to me when I told her I loved her. That meant she had someone else. Or at least someone who loved her and she loved them back.

The ache grew into a fire, and I wanted to punch something.

"Sorry," she said. "Family thing."

"You have a family?" I asked, looking for the first time at her left hand. "You're not wearing a ring."

"Family doesn't always mean a marriage," she said, crossing her arms over her chest. "I just came to tell you why I freaked out. Now that you know, you can go back to forgetting I exist."

She moved to go around me, but I placed a hand on her arm, stopping her.

"I didn't mean to hurt you," I said. "Will you call me?"

Looking at my hand on her arm, she turned her eyes up to me, and the shine in them confused me. There were tears just waiting to fall, but she had a firm hold on them.

"Goodbye, Heath," she said, stepping past me and opening the door.

"Fuck," I mumbled once she had been gone for a bit.

CHAPTER NINE

Dani...

By the time I got to my car, the tears were coming in rivulets down my cheeks. I had no idea how I held them at bay until I was out of the stadium, but thankfully, Heath wouldn't see me cry over him. He would never know the gallons of tears he'd caused. Not because of anything he did but because I knew I couldn't ever have him. At least not in any meaningful way.

Sure, I had a small piece of him in our daughter, but it wasn't the same. There had never been anyone else I ever wanted. I just couldn't jump from one prison to another. Whether he would be as controlling as my parents wasn't something I was willing to test, and when I threw in Paisley, the fierce protectiveness within me expanded. It wasn't worth tempting fate.

I pulled in a breath, held it, and then blew it out before pulling my phone back out and calling my aunt.

"What was that about?" she asked when she answered.

"Sorry," I said. "Is Paisley there?"

"Hang on," she said, then passed the phone to my daughter.

"Mama," she said. "You sound sad. It's my birthday tomorrow, and you're always happy on my birthday. Did I make you sad?"

"No, baby," I said, unable to stop the smile. "I was just kind of in the middle of something and couldn't talk right then."

"Auntie said you were working on my cake," she said. "Did you get it finished?"

"I sure did," I said. It wasn't a lie, just the timing of it wasn't quite the truth. "I had to go get some extra stuff, but I'm heading back to pick up the cake now. Did you do your homework?"

"I'm too young to have homework," she said. "You must be really old if you got homework when you were little like me."

"I must be too old," I said, not bothering to hide the laugh that escaped. "But it's still important to study. What book are you reading now?"

"Mrs. Kennedy gave me one for my birthday," she said, and I braced for it to be something that crossed another line. "She said she read it when she was in second grade. It's called *Charlotte's Web*."

I breathed a sigh of relief, thanking whatever higher power in the universe had made sure that my little chat with the principal had done the trick.

"Sounds like a good book," I said.

"Have you read it?" she asked.

"I might have," I said. "But you know how forgetful I am."

"Yeah," she said, then laughed. "Because you're old."

"I've gotta get going," I said. "Can't pick up your cake if I don't get to the bakery."

"Okay, bye," she said, then disconnected the call.

"Stinker," I mumbled, then shifted to put my seatbelt on and damn near jumped out of my skin. "What the fuck are you doing here?" I asked.

"I didn't like how we left things," Heath said. "Who was that?"

"Are you stalking me?" I asked.

"No," he said, but didn't budge from where he was, leaning on the open window of my car. "Who were you talking to?"

"Why does it matter?"

"Dani," he said, and I could hear the exasperation in his voice.

"Look," I said. "It isn't anything for you to worry about. I really need to get going."

"How old is she?" he asked, and my mouth fell open. "Is she mine?"

Oh God, I thought.

CHAPTER TEN

H eath...

"I've gotta get going," she said. "Can't pick up your cake if I don't get to the bakery."

Whoever she was talking to must have said goodbye, because I heard her mumble, "Stinker."

She jumped when she saw me at her window. I'd followed her out, far enough back that she wouldn't see me, but she wasn't paying attention, so I could have been right on her heels. I wanted to hold her and tell her everything would be fine, but I had to know who had called her. I didn't want to wait for Duncan to get the scoop, so I went to the source.

The conversation she'd had wasn't with an adult, or at least I didn't think it was. The more she spoke, the more anxious I got, and when she got toward the end of the call, I knew she was talking to a child, likely hers.

"I didn't like how we left things," I said. "Who was that?"

"Are you stalking me?" she asked, and I heard both anger and fear in her voice.

"No," I said. I was leaning on her window, so she was stuck unless she decided to ignore the chance of an injury to me. "Who were you talking to?"

"Why does it matter?"

"Dani," I said, and didn't bother to hide my frustration.

"Look," she said. "It isn't anything for you to worry about. I really need to get going."

"How old is she?" I asked, having looked at the interior of her car. "Is she mine?"

I guessed a daughter judging by the amount of pink sitting in the back seat, and her reaction told me I was right.

"I can't do this right now," she said, starting her car.

"Danielle Louise Lloyd," I said. "Do we have a child together? If we do, why have you never bothered to tell me?"

Her hand was over her mouth, her breathing shallow. I knew from experience that she was gonna lose whatever food she'd consumed, so I pulled the door open to give her room to get sick, which she did. I grabbed her hair, holding it out of the way of her emotional release until she'd finished. How many times had I done the same thing when she'd been so upset about things she wouldn't tell me about? It was the best I could do back then, but things were different now. She didn't have to hide anything from me anymore. She was an adult, and so was I. Her family had nothing to hold against her anymore.

"Hey," I said when she sat back up. "Come back inside with me. Let's get you cleaned up before you go pick up that cake."

"I can't," she said, choking on the words. "I promised myself I wouldn't make her relive my life."

43

"Dani, please," I begged, tipping her eyes up to mine. "Let me help, at least for this."

She nodded and slid out of the car to lean against the back door. I reached in and turned it off, taking the keys and grabbing them and her purse, handing them to her. I snatched the phone off the front seat and shoved it in my pocket before shutting the door.

"Come on," I said, putting my arm around her shoulders.

Her hand flew up to her face, covering it just as I looked over and saw someone with their phone out. Not even thinking, I moved her behind me and reached out to grab it from the guy's hands.

"Hey, you can't..."

I deleted the picture, scrolled through several more he'd taken, deleting those as well, then went to his trash and emptied it to ensure everything was gone before I turned the phone off.

"You can't—"

"Yes, I can," I said, letting the full force of my anger come through my voice. "I might be a public figure, but *she* is not. If I see anything about her online anywhere, I'll find you and you'll pay. Do you understand?"

Whether it was my size—towering over him by half a foot—or the fact that I had dirt smudged on my uniform and my eye black was likely running along my cheeks from the sweat, he blinked, gaping like a fish while I waited. Finally, after running through whatever scenarios were going through his head, he nodded and mumbled a soft, "Sorry."

I took Dani's phone and snapped a picture of the guy, and when he went to protest, I simply stuffed the phone in my back pocket and guided her toward the stadium.

CHAPTER ELEVEN

D**ani...**
"Yes, I can," Heath said, and I could hear how pissed he was. "I might be a public figure, but *she* is not. If I see anything about her online anywhere, I'll find you and you'll pay. Do you understand?"

The guy said something, but I couldn't make it out and didn't care to try. Heath shifted around me again, but then he was moving me toward the stadium again. I kept my face buried in his chest, my hand on my face, not wanting to see anyone else. The noise of the crowd grew the closer we got. I was afraid I'd be shoved away from him, so I clung to his jersey with my fist, one on his chest and another on his back.

"Heath," I heard a man say and felt him nod before steering me again to a quieter place.

The noise lowered, nearly muffled completely, until he turned again. I heard a door shut, and Heath stopped. His arm rubbed up and down my back, and he pushed me away from him slightly. I blinked, realizing we were in a small room. Looking up at him, his face was contorted in a mix of confusion, pain, and anger. I wasn't sure which was more prominent or aimed at me directly.

"Dani," he said, rubbing his hands up and down my arms. "Talk to me, baby."

I opened my mouth, but nothing came out. I closed it and turned from him, finding a chair, then sitting down. Taking a deep breath, I let it out slowly, then tipped my head up to look at him. He hadn't moved from the door like he feared I'd run if he wasn't blocking the exit.

"I didn't want you to know," I said, and he sagged back. "Not because I didn't trust you. Please don't think that. I just couldn't tie myself to you then. I'd have felt guilty keeping you from your dream. It wouldn't be fair. To you, me, or Paisley."

"Paisley," he said, and it was a reverent sound.

"Yeah," I said. "There was never going to be another name for her. She'd been Paisley since our first time together."

"If she would've been a boy?" he asked, and I nodded. His sigh was almost one of contentment. I stood up and went to him—not like it was far—just a couple of steps. "How old is she?" he asked when I reached him.

"Her birthday is tomorrow," I said. "She'll be seven."

"Seven years," he said, and there was sadness in his voice.

"I'm so sorry," I said, apologizing again. "I should have reached out to you, but I couldn't chance it. You would have dropped everything..."

"Of course, I would have," he said, heat in his voice. "I would have been here in a minute, damn the rest of the world."

"And I couldn't do that to you," I said, pressing my hand to the middle of his chest. "You had a career to think about, and a distraction of a child would have gotten in the way."

"But—"

"No," I said, my voice firm now. "Heath, I couldn't do that to any of us. Paisley would have been a distraction, and if my parents had found out before she was born, they'd have hauled me home and kept me a prisoner. You know how Daddy is. He would have been ashamed and wanted to hide me away. Instead, I took that away from them and stood on my own."

"I would have helped you," he said.

"Aunt Cindi did that," I said. "She was everything I needed in a support person. She gave me the choice of what I wanted to do, saying she would help me with whatever I decided. She encouraged me to at least reach out to you and let you know, but I told her it would just be a disruption."

"But it's been years," he said.

"It just got away from me," I said. "Running into you brought me right back to the morning I first thought I was pregnant. All the fears I'd had then just slammed into me and I panicked."

His eyes were shiny, as if he were trying not to cry. I watched as he swallowed several times, the Adams Apple in his throat bobbing.

"I really am sorry," I said. "It's just been so long I didn't even think about it. Not until yesterday."

"Why yesterday?"

"She asked why she didn't have a daddy," I said, and the words looked like they physically hurt him. "She said her teacher said it was my fault."

"It is," he said, and it was my turn to be injured by words. "Sorry," he said. "That wasn't fair. You were a kid. Fuck, we both were."

"Yeah," I said. "I told her that you were busy."

"I'd have made time," he said.

I just nodded. There really wasn't a way to fix everything I'd messed up, but I wanted to. God, I wanted to go back in time and tell him the morning I peed on that stick and got the two pink lines.

"I should have called," I said. "I know that. I've had years to make that call, but I've just gotten more and more used to it just being the two of us. It wasn't because I didn't want you to know. It's just..."

There really wasn't a way to explain all the emotions, thoughts, and everything that had gone through me. Hell, I couldn't explain the feelings still going through me.

CHAPTER TWELVE

H**eath...**

The tiny room was suffocating me. Everything Dani had said was like another cut. If someone could die from a million paper cuts, I was on my way to that slow and torturous death. I had a child, a little girl, and Dani had named her Paisley. Paisley Jane or Hunter Emory. Those were the names we'd picked out after our very first time.

We were barely sixteen the first time we had sex. Both of us were virgins. Of course, I fucked everything up by coming just from a quick stroke of her hands on me. I felt like an absolute fool, but she'd assured me it was fine. As if she'd known exactly how to comfort me and to help me not feel as bad.

Finally, though, we'd gotten the condom on, gotten her aroused enough that she wanted to try, and when I'd slid inside, it felt like I'd found my own personal heaven. Not in some sappy way, but like she was the missing piece of my entire world. I never wanted to be anywhere else. It was truly making love with her every single time. No matter how many times, no matter how many ways, each and every time, it felt the same—absolute heaven.

In the afterglow, we'd had a heart-to-heart talk about our futures. She was going to go away for school after she graduated, and that was non-negotiable. When she told me it was to escape her family, I'd laughed. Now I understood, though. All the little things I thought were just a little odd turned out to be glaring red flags.

Her dad was a preacher and one of those Southern Baptist types. Fire and brimstone were always a topic when he was in the pulpit. Thou shalt not... Whatever it was, if it was fun or felt good or could lead to anything other than the uptight and rigid picture-perfect façade he portrayed, you couldn't do it.

Dani sang in the choir in the loft above the pulpit every Sunday. She was the one I was worshipping in that building, and the fact that I wasn't struck dead by a bolt of lightning just proved that miracles still happened. But she was perfect in every way there could be. Except she lied, ghosted me and the whole fucking town, and robbed me of seven years of my daughter's life.

"Say something," she said, bringing me back to the here and now.

"It's a lot," I said, then swallowed. "It's just a lot to take in all at once."

"I know," she said. "Let's put a pin in it and pick it back up later."

"Not a chance," I said, turning to her. "I've missed seven years of Paisley's life. I'm not willing to miss anymore."

"What do you mean?" she asked, and I heard the fear in her voice.

"I'm not gonna try to take her away from you," I said.

"I'd never do that. But I do want to meet her and get to know her. I think I'm owed at least that."

"You're not gonna waltz in there and declare your fatherhood on her birthday," she said, and this time, instead of fear, it was anger I heard.

"That's not what I meant," I said. "But I want to meet her. Let me get cleaned up, and we can go to your place to meet her now."

"No," she said, and the finality in the one word nearly buckled my knees.

"Dani," I began.

"I need to get her prepared for that," she said. "I'm not going to fuck up her birthday. I'll talk to her after her party, let her know that I've talked to you and that you'd like to meet her. She gets to decide."

"Let me come to her party," I suggested.

"Because that wouldn't be a disaster." She scoffed. "Look," she continued. "I get that you want to meet her, and I want you to. But you have to let me do this my way. You don't know her. Let me ease her into this. Please?"

The word please and the begging I saw in her eyes drove home the fact that Paisley wasn't something I could just take. She was a person, and I had to trust Dani to let me meet her the right way.

"What if I came to dinner tonight?" I asked. "Not as her dad, but maybe as an old friend. Someone you haven't seen in a while?"

I could see the wheels turning in her head, and when she came out with a soft, "Okay," I let go of the breath I'd been holding. "But no mention of her dad. At all."

"Of course," I said.

"I do need to go," she said. "I need to tell my aunt about this, figure out what I'm gonna make, and—"

Her phone rang, and we both jumped because it was in my back pocket. I pulled it out and handed it to her.

"Margie," she said. "I'm on the way to grab the cake." It was a short conversation before she disconnected. "I do have to go."

"Let me shower really quick," I said. "I'll walk you out."

"I'm not so sure," she said. "The last time you were out there with me, it didn't go so well."

"Yeah," I said. "I need you to send me that picture I took. Security needs to be made aware of him."

"Okay," she said.

"My number's still the same," I added. "I know you don't want me to walk you out, but let me have security do it."

"Because that won't draw more attention," she said, sarcasm dripping from each word. "I'll just walk out with some other people, slip into my car, and then head out."

I wanted to argue, but I just couldn't come up with anything valid.

"I'll send the picture and the address when I get home," she said. "Does six work for dinner?"

"Sure," I said. "What can I bring?"

"Nothing," she said. "I gotta go, though."

"Yeah," I said, though I wasn't keen on her leaving my side.

"I'll send it to you," she said, but I didn't know if she was trying to convince me or herself.

CHAPTER THIRTEEN

Dani...

I stopped at the grocery store before going to the bakery, picking up some boxed lasagna and garlic bread, along with a salad in a bag. I could cook, but I didn't want to try and do that, along with everything else I needed to get done. Besides, my nerves were shot, and a mindless meal was all I could handle.

"You're back," Margie said as I walked in the back door. "That man this morning said for you to call him."

"I saw him," I said, not really wanting to get into this whole thing with her, but not wanting to seem rude. "He's an old friend from back home. It just startled me to see him here."

"Well," she said, a sparkle in her eyes. "He was pretty to look at, if nothing else."

I let out a laugh because she was right. Heath had always been pretty to look at. God, even when we were little, everyone doted on him. The blond hair that darkened as he got older, with just enough waves to it, gave him that angelic appearance. Last time I'd seen him, that killer smile, with the dimple that only showed up when he was giving a true smile, had melted my heart. Now, though, with more than half a dozen years gone by, the hair was darker still, and with the short beard and mustache, he likely had to fight off women.

"Not gonna argue," I said. "I came to pick up the cake. I've got frozen food in the car, so I can't stay long."

"Who is he?" she asked just as Terri came through the swinging doors.

"Oh, hi," she said when she saw me. "You coming back in?"

"Just picking up the cake," I said. "Gotta make it quick. Don't want the frozen food to melt while I'm in here."

"Let me help you," she said, stepping into our walk-in cooler.

"Well?" Margie asked, and it took me a minute to remember what she'd asked earlier.

"Just an old friend," I said, not wanting to add anything more.

"You said that," she said, sounding miffed.

"I'll tell you later," I said, taking the cake from Terri and backing out of the kitchen. Last thing I needed was her going on a hunting trip and finding out who Heath was and that he was a professional baseball player.

"He's coming here?" Aunt Cindi asked, her voice pitching up.

"I didn't want it to just be the three of us," I said, keeping my voice low.

Paisley was home from school and sitting at the table finishing her journaling for the day. I'd just put the lasagna in the bottom oven and was putting the Texas toast onto the cookie sheets to go in the top oven once the lasagna was almost done.

"But the house isn't guest-ready," she complained.

"Which is fine," I said. "Besides, you have the better oven."

"Go get your dining room ready," she said. "Then, take a shower and get yourself ready. I'll make sure Paisley finishes her homework, and we'll bring dinner over when it's time."

"I don't need a shower," I argued, but she put her hand on her hip and gave me a look I knew not to argue with. "Okay, fine," I said. "But he's gonna show up here, 'cause I gave him your address, not mine."

"Then I'll bring the dinner over and wait for him to show up and bring him over then," she said.

"I'll just text him and tell him to come to my house," I said.

"Mama," Paisley said, standing in the doorway between the kitchen and dining room. "How come you sound upset?"

"I'm just a bit tired," I said. "And running into an old friend has kinda flustered me. He's coming to dinner, so I had to do a bunch to get ready for that. Besides, Auntie is being mean and telling me we have to eat at our house. She's also making me take a shower."

"Mom," Paisley said, drawing the word out. "There's nothing wrong with taking a shower. You don't wanna stink when meeting with friends. That's what you always tell me."

"You're right," I said with a chuckle. "Maybe you should take a shower, too. Don't want to stink when you meet someone new, do you?"

"Ugh," she said, rolling her eyes. "Fine. But I'm not gonna like it."

I kissed her head, then headed out the side door of my aunt's to walk across the short space to go into my own house to get ready for the night I didn't want to have.

CHAPTER FOURTEEN

Heath...

After Dani left, I'd walked back out to the dugout to check with the manager and make sure I was good to bail. He gave me the go-ahead, so I grabbed my street clothes and took a quick shower to get the surface shit off before heading to the car to drive out to my condo. I wanted to take a good shower, find something nice to wear, and pick up a bottle of wine and some flowers. Making a good first impression was important to me, even if she was just a little girl.

When I got home, I stripped on the way to my room, throwing everything into the laundry basket before stepping into the shower. I was glad Duncan had gotten a place with a decent shower because I hated those tub-only things. They just weren't big enough, and I always felt closed in.

I showered again, making sure I hadn't missed anything the first time around, then shut the water off and dried off. I pulled out a decent pair of slacks and a button-down short-sleeved shirt. It wasn't hot yet, but the handful of times I'd come to play in Arizona, the heat was unbearable. I knew once the late spring months came and the summer started to sizzle, I wouldn't want to wear anything more than I had to.

Once I dressed, I grabbed my phone, keys, and wallet and headed out to the car. It had been nice that Duncan worked to get the car out for me. Using a rental for an entire season was just a stupid use of money. I didn't like that it had to be shipped, but it was cheaper than either a rental or buying one to have here. Thankfully, it had arrived the day after I did, so I hadn't been without it but for a couple days.

Using the GPS on my phone, I found a shop that had ready-made bouquets, so I headed that way and picked up one with yellow roses and another with pink. Having seen all the pink in the back seat, I took it as a sign that my girl liked the color. I knew Dani loved yellow roses, or at least she did back in school. The next stop was a wine shop, fortunately, in the same little shopping area. Since I didn't know what she was making, I opted for a light rosé, which would go with almost everything.

Having my gifts in hand, I pulled up the text from the local number Dani had sent the information from, seeing she sent me two addresses. Reading back through the texts, I saw that the second address was her house and that she was originally gonna have me go to her aunt's place. I'd just started out of the parking lot when Duncan called.

"Hey," I said when I answered the phone through the car's system.

"I have some information," he said. "You want me to send it to you?"

"Hold on to it for now," I said. "Let me get through a dinner tonight, and I'll reach out to you tomorrow after the game."

"You want the CliffsNotes?" he asked.

"She has a daughter," I said. "She's mine, and I'm meeting her tonight."

"Oh, okay," he said, sounding like I'd stolen his thunder.

"Yeah," I said. "She came to the game and talked to me."

"Should I be drawing up any paperwork for custody?"

"No," I said with more force than was probably necessary. "No, she's been open with the information. She's letting me come to meet her tonight. We're holding off on telling her who I am, but I was adamant I meet her as soon as possible. So an impromptu dinner at her place is happening."

"You just tell me what you want," he said.

"For now, just hold," I said. "If I need anything, I'll call."

"If you're sure," he said, and I knew he was just giving me plenty of chances to change my mind on the things he'd offered.

"I am," I said.

"All right," he said.

"Thanks," I replied. "I appreciate the fast turnaround you did on this."

"I hope the night goes well," he said.

"Talk soon," I replied, then disconnected the call.

It didn't take long for me to get to the neighborhood where she lived, and the little houses along it were adorable. Not big, but decent sized. I didn't know if she was renting or buying, but either way, I'd be giving her some help financially, if nothing else. Pulling up in front of the place, I took a deep breath before turning the car off. I grabbed the roses and wine and opened the door, ready to meet my baby for the first time.

CHAPTER FIFTEEN

Dani...

Aunt Cindi had brought over the lasagna when it was finished, along with the frozen toast for me to cook in my oven. She said she'd bring the salad when she came back with Paisley. She was just gonna put her in the bath after she left, so I handed her a bag with a change of clothes for her after she was done.

Half an hour later, the knock at the door startled me. Having just pulled the toast from the oven, and turning it off, I walked to the front door. Aunt Cindi and Paisley hadn't come back yet, so I figured it was them. When I pulled the door open, though, it was Heath, holding so many roses it was ridiculous and a bottle of wine that looked expensive. Not that I would know how expensive wine was because I didn't really drink it.

"Oh," I said when I saw him. "I didn't realize it was so late."

"I think I'm a little early," he said. "Is that okay?"

"Um, yeah," I said, stepping back to let him in. "Let me call my aunt and see what's taking them so long."

I'd barely gotten the words out when Paisley pushed the door back open and came in like the hurricane she was.

"Mama," she said, then stopped cold, looking warily at Heath.

"Paisley," I said, moving to her side. "This is my friend, Heath. We've known each other since we were about your age."

"Hi," she said, not moving from my side.

I didn't know what to expect from Heath. His eyes widened for a moment, but he quickly schooled his features and put that smile I always loved on his face.

"It's a pleasure to meet you, Paisley," he said, holding out the bunch of pink roses. "I got these for you. I had to guess the color. Did I guess right?"

She nodded, a smile gracing her lips, and I realized how much she looked like her dad when she smiled. It nearly stopped my heart because he'd been true to his word so far in not pushing the "dad" card immediately.

"Do you wanna take those and put them in a vase, sweetie?" Aunt Cindi asked, and I looked at her and smiled.

"Okay," she said, taking the flowers offered and skirting around Heath toward the kitchen.

"These are for you," he said, handing me the other bunch. "You still like yellow roses, right?"

"I do," I replied, pushing my nose into them and inhaling the sweet scent. "I'm surprised you remembered."

"I remember everything," he said, and the sultry tone of his voice sent a shiver down my spine.

It took me a good minute to regain my composure. All the while, he just stood there, watching me, like he was trying to memorize everything about me.

"Um," I stammered, finally finding my voice. "Come in. Dining room is this way."

We walked into the dining area, and Paisley and Aunt Cindi were just putting the flowers in the middle of the table I'd set. My aunt had also brought out another vase to put my roses in. The salad sat in a bowl on the table, along with the lasagna and a plate of toast.

"Should I open the wine?" Heath asked.

"I don't think I'll have any," I said, wanting to keep my senses about me.

"Can I have wine?" Paisley asked.

"Let me see," Heath said, looking at her intensely. "Do you have your ID? Because we have to make sure you're at least twenty-one before we can serve you any."

She giggled, then said, "I don't have any of that. I'm only seven. Well, tomorrow I'll be seven."

"I guess you're out of luck, then," he said. "Would you like some?" he asked my aunt.

"That would be lovely," she said. "Why don't you come with me to open it and find some glasses."

"Of course," he said, turning to look at me before following her around the corner.

"Mommy," Paisley said, looking at me. "He has one blue eye and one green eye, like me. Isn't that cool?"

I hadn't even thought about the fact that they shared that gene. I mean, it made sense, and it was something I'd always loved about Heath. Still, the fact I didn't make that connection was wild.

"That's pretty neat," I said.

Just then, Heath and Aunt Cindi came back from the kitchen with the open bottle of wine and four wine glasses. I looked at them, saw that my aunt brought a bottle of apple juice, and relaxed.

"I thought we'd make a toast," Heath said as he set the glasses down at each place setting. Again, my anxiety ratcheted up. "To old friends reconnecting," he said as he poured wine into two glasses. My aunt poured the juice into the other two, handing one to Paisley and the other to me. When she picked up the glass of wine, she held it out.

"To old friends," I said, clinking my glass with my daughter and then my aunt. I paused a moment before clinking it with Heath. He smiled and took a small sip of the wine.

"This looks good," he said. "Where should I sit?"

CHAPTER SIXTEEN

H**eath...**

Lasagna was definitely outside my meal plan, but it was spring, I was good on weight, and having dinner with my daughter meant I would eat anything that was served. The meal reminded me of what my mama would make when we were growing up, minus the salad. I think the first time I actually ate a salad was when I went out to eat with Dani for the first time.

Paisley told everyone where to sit, so I ended up next to Dani, her aunt across the table, and my daughter kitty-corner from me. We'd moved the flowers to the end of the table so we could all see each other. It took a while for her to warm up to me, which was fine. Meant she probably wasn't willing to walk off with just anyone, and I was glad about that.

"What do you do for a job?" Paisley asked about half an hour into the meal.

"I play baseball," I said.

"That's not a real job," she said.

"It is," I said. "I can take you to a game if you want. If it's okay with your mom, of course."

"I don't believe you," she said, and I could see my own stubbornness in her. "Mama, tell him playing baseball isn't a job."

"Paisley," Dani said. "It really is his job. And he's really good at it."

Her praise did something to me, and I slid my hand over to her thigh. She flinched and pulled away, so I put my hand back on my leg, noting her skittish nature. I didn't remember her being this tense in school, but maybe being a mom or being away from her family had changed her. That was something I wanted to get to the bottom of.

"...can we go?"

I'd been so in my head I'd missed whatever it was Paisley had been saying, so I asked her to repeat the question.

"I asked when we can go," she said. "To the game."

"That's up to your mom," I said. "I can't make those decisions for you. It's her job."

It was a little dig at being unable to be a dad to her, but it wasn't so blatant that it would be obvious.

"Let's get through your birthday party first," Dani said.

"Oh," Paisley said. "Can you come to my party tomorrow? Mama, can he come to the party?"

"I don't think that'll work," Dani said. "He's really busy right now since the season is just starting. We'll plan a time to watch him play soon, though, okay?"

"Please," she begged, drawing out the word for nearly half a minute.

"Paisley," I said. "Your mom said no. Don't beg."

She looked at me like I'd slapped her, and then her bottom lip started to tremble. Before I realized it, she was dashing from the table and down the hallway toward what I assumed were the bedrooms.

"Great," Dani said, slapping her napkin on the table. She glared at me like I'd done the most unthinkable thing before heading down the hallway to follow her.

I looked at her aunt, unsure what I'd said or done that was so terrible.

"She gets sensitive when someone tells her no," the woman explained. "Dani works hard to make sure she isn't spoiled, but she's also specific about how she admonishes her so she doesn't throw a fit like this."

"I didn't know," I said. "None of the guys who had kids on the Blues had that happen. I've been around a lot of kids, and they all just took a no as a no. Begging doesn't happen. At least not when they were around me or the rest of the team."

"Paisley's been an only child her whole life," Aunt Cindi said. "She knows what she is and isn't allowed to do, but she does try to push things. Dani's amazing with her, though. So patient, explaining things to her in kid-friendly words, but also treating her like her own person, which she is."

"I guess I better work harder at this if I'm gonna be in her life," I said.

"Yeah," she said. "She needs a dad, but not one who is so totally different from her mom. At least not at this stage."

"Do you have any tips?" I asked.

"Follow Dani's lead," she said. "She knows the best way to get through to Paisley, even when she's being a pain."

I nodded, because what else could I do? I wasn't her dad in the traditional sense. I mean, yeah, she was my blood, but there was more to being a parent than biology. There were a handful of guys on the team who had adopted kids, and they were more present in their lives than some of the guys I'd grown up with. This whole thing was such a crazy whirlwind that I needed to remember that I was the new person in this situation, and I didn't know all the secret codes to get the outcome I wanted. On the field, I knew what to do, but this was foreign. Not so much as to be impossible to learn, but it would take time.

CHAPTER SEVENTEEN

Dani...

"Great," I said because a cranky Paisley was not what I needed tonight. I was already on edge having Heath in my house. He didn't know my daughter, and him thinking he could come in here and just parent her without blowback was bullshit. I told him as much in the look I gave him, then headed down the hall after my daughter to see if I could mitigate the trauma.

"Go away," Paisley said as I walked into her room. "He's a stupid boy who doesn't know anything. Why did you let him come to dinner?"

"Baby girl," I said, sitting on the edge of her bed that she'd flopped onto. "Come here." She looked at me over her shoulder, then shifted and sat up, climbing into my lap, tears staining her cheeks. "Heath is an old friend I haven't seen in a really long time," I explained. "He surprised me by coming into the bakery this morning. I decided to invite him to dinner to catch up. I'm sorry he was short with you, though."

"Boys are dumb," she said, and I laughed.

"They sometimes are," I replied. "But calling someone dumb isn't nice, either. Would you like it if he said girls are dumb?"

"But girls are smart," she said.

"Boys can be, too," I replied.

"Is he your boyfriend?" she asked, and I was confused. "Macy's mom has a new boyfriend. Macy said that he's mean to her and won't let her do what she wants."

"I don't always let you do what you want," I tried, a little concerned about what was happening at her friend's house.

"I guess," she said. "But she said that he's been picking on her. Telling her she's dumb and needs to look pretty if she wants to have a boyfriend."

"Pretty isn't what good guys look for," I said. "But maybe I should talk to her mom and see if I can help a little. Would that be okay?"

"Don't tell her I told you," she said. "Macy said she isn't supposed to tell people."

"Do you remember the rules I told you about secrets?" I asked.

"Secrets are fine if they're about a surprise," she said. "But if you can't tell your mom. teacher, or another adult because someone will get into trouble, then it isn't a secret you should keep."

"Good job," I said, stroking her hair. "So, telling me is a good thing, right?"

"Yeah," she said. "So, how come he had to come to dinner tonight?"

And we were back on Heath, which was not a subject I wanted to discuss with my daughter at this time. Still, I needed to tell her something. I would just hold off on the whole truth until I could figure out a way to say it without it coming out like I'd been lying to her for her entire life.

"It's because it's the first time I've seen him in a while," I said.

"Did he used to be your boyfriend?" she asked.

"He did," I said.

"Is he gonna be your boyfriend again?"

"It's been a long time since we've seen each other," I said. "It's like we have to get to know each other again. Like he's a new person, even though I knew him before."

"Do you want him to be your boyfriend?" she asked.

"Sweetheart," I said. "Why are you so concerned about boyfriends right now?"

"I dunno," she said.

"Is someone telling you that you need to get a boyfriend?" I asked. Because if so, heads would roll.

"Mama," she said, looking up at me.

"What is it, baby?" I asked.

"I don't want you to forget about me if you get a boyfriend," she said.

"Nothing could make me forget about you, baby," I said. "You're the most important person in my life. If someone wants me to give you up, forget about you, or anything like that, they can hit the road. Ain't gonna happen."

"Really?" she asked.

"For sure," I said. "Pinky promise."

I held my little finger out for her to hook hers into, which she did, then smiled.

"Can't never break a pinky promise," she said. "If you do, your pinky will fall off, and that's gross."

I laughed because what else could I do?

"You wanna come back to the table?" I asked.

"No," she said, sullen.

"Why not?"

"'Cause he'll think I'm dumb," she said.

"I don't think so," I said. "Tell you what. You come out and I'll let you have some of the extra treats I got for tomorrow. That sound good?"

"Not my cake," she said, her eyes big.

"Not the cake," I replied. "But I got some extra goodies, and I think I might have enough to let you have one. In fact, I think there might be enough for everyone to have one."

"Really?" she asked.

"Did you think I wouldn't bring dessert for dinner?"

"Not if your boyfriend was coming," she said, drawing the word boyfriend out entirely too dramatically for my taste.

"You are ridiculous," I said, kissing her head. "Now, come help me with the tarts."

"Tarts?"

The way her voice rose was comical, and I just had to laugh again, pulling her up to follow me back to the kitchen.

CHAPTER EIGHTEEN

H eath...
　　When I heard footsteps coming back from down the hall, I felt a bit better, but it wasn't until I actually saw both Paisley and Dani coming that I really relaxed.

"Hey," I said to Paisley.

"I don't want to talk to you right now," she said, and damn if she wasn't just as feisty as her mama.

"I just wanted to apologize," I said. "I shouldn't have talked to you like that. Can you forgive me?"

I didn't know whether it was what I said or how I said it, but she paused and looked at me, tilting her head in a way that reminded me of Dani when she was working out her math problems. That's when I realized she had my eyes. The different colors didn't quite stand out when I first met her, but the way the light was in the dining room and the angle she held her head, it was clear as day.

She must have seen something in my face because she asked, "Why are you looking at me like that?"

"Sorry," I said. "I just noticed that you've got eyes like mine."

"See, Mama," she said, sounding damn proud of herself. "I told you they were the same."

"They sure are, baby," she said.

The way she bit her lower lip did something to me, and damn if I didn't wanna touch her again. All the things I'd missed by not knowing started to fester in me, but I quashed it. She'd said she did it because she didn't want to burden me. She wanted me to have the life I'd always wanted. The life she said I deserved. I wanted a life with her, though. From the moment she first said she'd go out with me, that's all I cared about outside baseball.

"We're gonna get the tarts," she said, sashaying her little self into the kitchen.

Cindi and I had already cleared the table, putting the lasagna into the fridge, along with the leftover salad and toast. Then she'd said goodnight to me and to let Dani know she'd gone home.

"Can I help?" I asked Dani.

"We've got it," she said, her voice a little softer than it was earlier. "Where's Aunt Cindi?"

"She and I cleaned up, then she said she was going home," I said.

She gave a sigh, then followed our daughter into the kitchen. I couldn't help but admire the view. It was now just the three of us, and I wondered whether Dani had said anything to Paisley about me being her dad. It wasn't something I was gonna mention until I'd had a chance to confirm that with Dani. Much as I wanted to stake my claim, I knew it wasn't the right time.

"Do you want ice cream?" I heard Paisley shout from the kitchen.

"No, thank you," I said, getting up to head in that direction.

"You don't want ice cream?" she asked, her eyes wide.

"I have to make sure I'm careful with what I eat," I said.

"Why?"

"Well," I said. "I play baseball, so I have to make sure I can still do all the things I need to do to help my team with their games."

"Ice cream gives me energy," she said. "Don't you want energy so you can run really fast?"

"Much as I'd like ice cream to work like that for me, it doesn't," I said. "It makes me slow. Especially if I eat it right before a game."

"Do you have a game tonight?" she asked, and I smiled.

"I already played my game today," I explained.

"So, you can have ice cream then," she said. I wish logic in the real world worked like her thought process seemed to.

"Thank you for trying," I said. "But that won't work."

"You gonna eat a tart?" she asked.

I had to bite the inside of my cheek to keep the laugh at her choice of words. Dani's mom had said she was a tart when she found out we were having sex. And if I had my way, I'd definitely be at least sampling the tart that was the mother of my child.

"I'll have a small piece," I said.

"They're just a tart," she said, her hands on her hips. "You can't have a piece of one. You gotta eat the whole thing."

I held my hands up in surrender, not really knowing how to answer her.

"Paisley," Dani said, and I looked from our daughter to her. "Let's get to the table and have dessert."

"Okay," she said, scooting around me.

"Sorry," Dani said.

"I don't mind," I said. "I'm just thankful to be here and see her. Thank you." She nodded, holding two plates, one in each hand, then looked to the counter where a third plate was. "I got it," I said, picking it up.

CHAPTER NINETEEN

Dani...

The tension had eased off after dinner, and by the time we ate dessert, it felt almost like a real family moment, or at least the ones I'd seen on television growing up. Certainly not my family, though. Those were all about appearances and making sure we had a picture-perfect look, no matter how rotten we were under the surface.

Paisley was yawning by the time she finished her tart, and with her party the following day, I knew she needed to head to bed. I said as much and she'd whined about not wanting to go until later, needing to stay up and ask all the questions about Heath and what he did playing baseball. When he looked at me after answering another question, I sort of gave him a look that said she needed to go to bed, and it likely wouldn't happen until he left. Unfortunately, he didn't get the clue.

"Sweetheart," I said, getting her to look at me. "You have your party tomorrow. If you don't wanna be a crank pot, you better get some sleep."

"But, Mom," she said, drawing the word out.

Heath cleared his throat but didn't say anything, thankfully.

"Paisley Jane," I said, my voice firm.

"Fine," she said with a sigh bigger than she was.

I waited for Heath to ask to assist, but he kept his mouth shut, so I excused us. My girl said goodnight, and we headed down the hall.

"We'll take showers in the morning," I said as I helped her change into her pajamas. "Thank you for being nice to my friend tonight."

"Are you gonna kiss him?" she asked. I needed to really have a talk with her about where all these kinds of questions were coming from, but not tonight.

"I don't think so," I said.

"Oh," she said, sounding a bit sad. "Don't you like him?"

"I like him just fine," I said. "But we haven't seen each other in years. He's almost a stranger to me now."

"Okay," she said, a yawn punctuating the word.

"Brush your teeth," I said, guiding her into the bathroom.

We finished the rest of her routine, got her tucked in, and she was out before I even got up off the edge of her bed. Now, though, I was left with her father in my house and nothing to distract us from each other or the million questions I was sure he'd have. Tucking my girl's hair behind her ear, I kissed her temple, then stepped out of her room, closing the door behind me.

Walking back toward the dining room where I'd left him, I startled a bit when he was standing right at the end of the hall.

"Sorry," he said, steadying me with a hand on my elbow. "I didn't mean to scare you."

"It's fine," I said, walking past him to sit on the couch. "We should talk."

He sat down near the other end of the couch, not quite too far, but not right next to me, either. I appreciated the fact that he gave me some space. Neither of us said anything for a few minutes, just sort of looking at each other, taking in the years that had passed since we'd last seen the other one.

"I'm sorry," I said, just as he asked, "When did you know?"

"Sorry," I said again.

"It's fine," he said. "When did you know you were pregnant?"

"Not until I'd been here for a couple of months," I replied. "I was never very regular, and with the stress of the move and basically cutting my family and friends off, I figured that was what was going on. When I started getting sick every morning, Aunt Cindi started asking me some questions and then brought home a test from the store. It lit right up almost immediately, so she took me to the doctor."

"Did they tell you when they thought you got pregnant?" he asked. "Or can they even do that?"

"They gave me a best guess," I said. "Probably the last time we were together. If not then, then the time or two before that."

"We were careful," he said.

"I know," I replied. "That's what I told them."

"It's not like we ever had a broken condom," he said. "At least I don't remember one."

"No," I said. "We didn't. But nothing is guaranteed to be foolproof."

"You're really good with her," he said, and I smiled at

his shifting gears. "She's amazing. Just as beautiful as her mama."

"And stubborn as her daddy," I said, biting my lip. "I wanted to tell you right away, but we'd wiped my phone. I didn't even know if you had the same number. I'm sure I could have found it, though."

"I wish you had," he said. "I would have come right away."

"I know," I said, looking down at my hands. I picked at my nail briefly before looking back up at him. "I'm sorry. I should have tried. I was just so scared you'd try to..."

I stopped my train of thought. This was Heath, not my dad. He'd never been so uptight about the way things looked or the impression he made to anyone else. He scooted closer, tipping my head up with a finger under my chin.

"I'm not your dad," he said, and it was like he'd read my mind. "I would have married you, but I wouldn't have forced you if you didn't want to."

"You would have had to give up your dream," I said, a tear slipping out before I could stop it. "I didn't want to derail your entire life because we somehow screwed up."

"Baby," he said, and the look in his eyes told me everything. The tears started in earnest, and he pulled me into his arms and held me, kissing the top of my head and telling me everything would be all right, even though nothing would.

CHAPTER TWENTY

Heath...

When she started to fall apart, I did the only thing I could, and that was to gather her to me and hold her while she cried. I didn't know if they were tears of sorrow, relief, anger, or something else. All I knew was that I would do anything to make them stop. It took a few minutes, and her cries were quiet, but her whole body shook with the sobs she wasn't vocalizing. Finally, though, she settled herself and pulled away from me, wiping her eyes with the back of her hand.

"I'm sorry," she said, her voice rough. "I haven't had a good cry about anything in a while. Oh, your shirt."

She began to brush against my chest, and I took her hand to stop her. If she kept touching me like that, I was going to have a hard time holding myself as a gentleman.

"I can always buy another shirt," I said. "Do you guys need anything? I mean, I need to catch up on child support at the very least."

"We're fine," she said, shaking her head.

"Hey," I said, tipping her head up again until she was

looking me in the eye. "I don't want to do it out of duty. I want to because it's the right thing to do. I'm not buying anything, or at least not trying to make it seem like that. But I do need to do what's right, as her dad."

She nodded, whether it was her agreeing with me or simply acknowledging the fact that I had a responsibility. Either way, I took it as a good sign.

"I have to figure out how to tell her," she said.

"Would you consider a counselor to help out?" I asked. "The team has those kinds of options available for the players. I could give you a list of names if you wanted to try that."

"She's not great with strangers," she said. "You probably noticed that when she got here."

"Maybe you could talk to one," I suggested. "Get some ideas on the best way to tell her or something?" She had a look on her face that I'd never seen before. It was like she was seeing me for the first time. "What?"

"Never would have thought you'd do anything like therapy," she said.

"It's important," I replied. "Honestly, mental health is just as important as physical health. Sometimes, it's more important. When your head isn't right, it doesn't matter how good you are. It'll screw your whole game up."

"Wow," she said.

"You do any therapy?" I asked.

"Yeah," she said. "I did some when I first got here. Then after I found out about Paisley, I needed more. Not because I wasn't happy but because it was all so overwhelming. Aunt Cindi was honestly a godsend. I never would have gotten through all of this without her."

"I'm glad she was here for you," I said.

"But you wish you were," she said, and I didn't argue. "I

really thought it was for the best. If I had let you know, I felt like you would've just left your dreams to come and rescue me. I didn't want that on my conscience. I couldn't have handled it if I had taken your dream away from you. I mean, look at you now. You're playing in the big leagues, just like you wanted to."

"I am," I agreed. "But I would have loved to be here for the first few years of her life."

"It was totally selfish of me," she began, but I stopped her with a look.

"You did what you thought was best," I said. "I can't fault you for that. You were in a position no one wanted you to be in. There were so many ways you could have handled this, but it was all your choice. I couldn't make you do anything you didn't want. I'm happy you kept her, though, because she is truly amazing."

"And so damn smart," she said.

"Which is all you," I replied. "You were the smartest kid in school. Top of the class in every way possible. I couldn't have asked for a better mother for my child."

"Mama."

I heard her small voice, and both Dani and I froze. The look in her eyes was one of fear and something else.

"Hey, baby," she said, getting up from the couch. "What're you doing up?"

"Umm," the little girl hummed, not looking at me but looking down at her feet.

"I'll be back," Dani said, then steered her down the hall.

"Fuck," I mumbled under my breath, running a hand down my face. I wondered whether she had heard any of our conversation.

CHAPTER TWENTY-ONE

Dani...
"Mama?"

I heard my girl before I saw her, and when I looked, she was confused, but that wasn't all I saw.

"Hey, baby," I said. "What are you doing up?"

"Umm," she said, then looked at the floor, and I knew what had happened.

"I'll be back," I said to Heath, then got up to take my girl to get her sorted.

When we got to her room, she was crying, and I just gathered her to me.

"It's okay, baby," I said.

"I didn't mean to," she said.

"Let's get you cleaned up," I said, taking her into the bathroom.

It had been almost a year since she'd last wet the bed. Back then, it was her transitioning to panties at night after taking forever to give up the pull-ups. We'd worked with her doctor to ensure there wasn't any medical reason for it, which there hadn't been, thankfully. I wondered if it was because Heath was here or if something else was upsetting her.

We got her out of her wet clothes, washed up, and into a pull-up, just for her peace of mind, before I stripped her bed, wiping up the last of the dampness from the plastic cover on her mattress. I put the sheets into her tub and would deal with them in the morning, then pulled out another set to get her back to bed.

"Mama," she said as I pulled the fitted sheet across the mattress pad, I'd already put down. "Is that man my daddy?"

I closed my eyes. Not because I was frustrated or anything but because I had wanted to have more time to figure out the best way to tell her. Deciding to not lie to her because I'd rather she knew the truth than find out later that I'd lied, I turned to her, having finished fitting her sheet on the bed.

"Come here," I said, sitting on her bed. She climbed up next to me, tucking into my side. "He is your dad, but he didn't know about you."

"Why not?"

"Because I didn't tell him," I said. "I should have, but I wanted him to have a life that wasn't forced on him."

"Doesn't he like me?" she asked, and I heard the tremble in her voice.

"Oh, baby," I said. "He likes you a lot. In fact, we were just talking about how we would tell you who he was."

"Is that why we have the same eyes?"

"It's one of the many things you got from him," I said.

"Is he gonna move in with us?" she asked.

"Baby," I said. "We have a lot of time to figure all that out. For now, though, you need to get to sleep. You don't want to be cranky at your party tomorrow, do you?"

"No," she said, then tipped her head up to me. "Can I go give him a hug?"

"You know what?" I asked.

"What?" she asked back.

"I think he'd really like that," I said.

She popped up and headed right out the door. I shook my head and got up to follow her.

CHAPTER TWENTY-TWO

Heath...
 I had no idea what had caused Paisley to wake up, and the way she looked so sad when she was standing there made me worried. Dani seemed to have everything figured out, though, so I sat and waited for her. I heard the water turn on down the hall and figured she'd had an accident. It took a while, and I heard their low voices coming from the other end of the house. I wondered what they were talking about.

Before I got too far up in my head, I heard footfalls coming down the hall. Looking up, I saw Paisley approaching me in a completely different pair of pajamas. I didn't have much time to react before she launched herself at me, arms outstretched. I caught her mid-flight, and she wrapped her arms around my neck.

"Hey, you," I said, confused at what was happening.

"Mama told me you're my daddy," she said, her small voice right next to my ears as her arms were tight around my neck.

"Sorry," Dani said as she came into view, but I just shook my head, unable to hide the smile from my face.

"I don't mind at all," I said, rubbing my girl's back. "But I think someone should probably get to bed so she is all rested up for her big day tomorrow. What do you say?" I asked as I eased my daughter from around my neck.

"Okay," she said, then kissed my cheek, surprising me. "I love you."

With those three little words, she was off my lap and on the run back to her room. I placed my palm over the place she'd kissed me, my eyes wide as I looked at her mom. Dani looked at me in shock, her eyes wide, her lower jaw damn near on the floor.

"Mama," we heard Paisley shout. "I need a blanket."

That shook Dani out of her shock, and she turned around and went back down the hall. I let my head fall back against the back of the couch, letting out a sigh. After all this time, I never thought that I would have Dani back in my life, let alone a daughter as wonderful as Paisley. My life was about to change in so many ways, and I couldn't be happier.

EPILOGUE

ALMOST TWO YEARS LATER...

Dani...

"You look beautiful, Mama," Paisley said.

"Thank you, baby," I said, kissing the top of her head. "You look beautiful yourself."

"Thank you," she said, spinning in her pink dress.

In two years, my life had changed in so many ways, and all of them were still baffling to me. Much as I wanted to build a family with Heath when we were in high school, I knew that I wouldn't hitch my wagon to a man if I couldn't make it on my own. Finding out I was pregnant nearly sent me into a downward spiral, and if it hadn't been for my aunt, I might have ended up in a way worse situation than I was.

Looking back, it was the best thing for me. The only downside was that Heath missed most of our daughter's early years. But he'd made up for it tenfold since he found out. He was such a good dad, and Paisley took to him without too much hesitancy. She was a great judge of character and the fact that she wasn't mad at me or him when she found out and simply accepted it was a testament to both her adaptiveness and his character.

"You ready?" Aunt Cindi asked as she poked her head in the door. "Oh, sweetheart. You are stunning."

I blushed because all the attention was too much.

"I'm ready," I said. "I think I've been ready for a while, actually."

"Well," she added. "If you don't hurry up, I'm afraid the groom is going to wear a hole in the floor with all the pacing he's been doing."

"We should probably go and rescue your dad," I told Paisley.

My aunt pushed the door open a little further, then held out her hand to me. I walked up and took it, giving it a squeeze.

"Thank you," I said, trying my best to keep the tears at bay.

"It has been my absolute pleasure," she said.

We walked down the hallway from the small room we'd been given to get ready in and headed to the banquet hall in the hotel. I'd never wanted a big wedding, even though my mother had tried to instill in me that princess mindset. I thought it was ridiculous to spend so much money on a single day that wasn't at all needed.

Thankfully, Heath was fine without having all the fuss. He asked about inviting my parents, but I was adamant that they were no longer a part of my life. My brother, his wife, and their little ones had come in, though, and it was fun to watch Paisley with her much younger cousins.

As we got closer to the room, butterflies began to fly in my belly, and I had to stop and center myself.

"Mama?" Paisley asked, looking at me with concern.

"It's okay," I said. "I just had to take a minute to realize this is all real."

She waited patiently, just watching me as I found my courage to walk into the next best part of my life.

HEATH...

The day started before the sun was even up, and I couldn't wait to get to the after-party. I was glad we'd chosen an early time for the wedding. The fact that I'd had to wait this long to make her my wife was hard enough. We spent nearly every day together, at least when I was in town. Going on the road had never been harder, but we'd made it work.

I'd wanted to marry her that first day, but she insisted that we get to know each other as we were rather than relying on our history to fuel our future. It was a good decision because we'd had some growing pains. Not like we were fighting, but more like life philosophy and things that could have been really big problems if we hadn't worked through them.

She'd also been pretty insistent that we were not gonna sleep together until after we'd said the two words that made us one. I respected her, but I'd be lying if I said it wasn't awful. There were a whole lot of long showers, but we were finally at that finish line, getting ready to finish our courtship and dive headlong into the rest of our lives.

When a hush came over the room, I froze, turning to look toward the door she was supposed to come through. It was a small affair, with just a few of our friends, along with her brother and his family. I held my breath as the door started to open.

Paisley stepped through the door first, her pink dress adorable, and she spun as she walked down the makeshift aisle set up for the occasion. When she got to me, she looked up and crooked her finger at me. I bent forward, and she kissed me on the cheek, much like she had that very first night.

Then, it was time. Jacob, her brother, started playing a light melody on the piano we'd had brought in, and I held my breath. When she stepped through the door, my knees almost buckled. If it wasn't for my best friend, Zac, I would've hit the floor. He gripped me under the arms until I was back to my steady self.

Never in my life did I think Dani was anything but beautiful, but when she walked through that door, her hair curling down past her shoulders, and the billowing skirt of her dress landing just at the floor, with the blue and purple and pink swirling throughout, I was blown away. It was like my body forgot how to exist, how to breathe, how my heart was supposed to beat. All of it was something that I had to try to remember.

My hand was at my mouth, holding in everything I wanted to say to her, all that I'd wanted to tell her from the moment I saw her in that bakery when I first came to town. This ceremony couldn't end soon enough because I wanted to pick her up, take her to our room, strip the lacy garment from her body, and reacquaint myself with the woman underneath.

Dani...

"I now pronounce you husband and wife," the preacher said. "You may kiss the bride."

The words were barely out of his mouth when Heath's was crashing into mine. It started out sweet, but when his tongue slid along the seam of my lips, I opened for him, and he was devouring me. I was giving as good as I got, having waited entirely too long for this moment. It wasn't a mistake to make us wait for the marriage to be intimate, but I'd be lying if I didn't say I regretted asking almost immediately. Now, though, the wait was more than worth it.

Applause broke the spell we'd fallen under, reminding us we weren't alone in the room. Pulling away from him was absolute torture, but I knew we needed to be present until we finished the celebration.

"Mama," Paisley said, looking up at me. "Daddy."

"Princess," Heath said, scooping her up in his arms.

Wrapping his other arm around me, he led us down the aisle to the back of the room, where our photographer stood waiting. She was taking pictures in rapid succession until we got closer.

"Let's get a few of the three of you," she said. "Then I'll take some of the bride and groom, and after that, each of you with Paisley. We can then do more with family and friends."

She got us set up in front of the backdrop she'd brought, and we were getting posed and shifted and all that, when all I wanted to do was get through whatever else was needed. When we were all done, we were taken over to the little cake that Margie made for us, which was beautiful. We cut the cake and fed it to each other, which did not include smashing it because I'd told him if he did that, I'd walk away, and we'd be over.

Finally, we were released to mingle with our guests, and the hugs were wonderful. Heath's friends from his old team and the new one were there. They were so tall, and their wives were beautiful. I felt a bit plain around them, but every time I looked at Heath, he had this stupid little grin on his face, and it made my self-esteem boost back up again.

When the night was coming to an end, Paisley came up to us, took each of our hands, and then smiled.

"What is it, baby?" I asked.

"Aunt Cindi is taking Uncle Jacob, Aunt Sarah, Josie, and Micah to her house," she said. "She said I was going with her, too. I just wanted to tell you guys I love you and goodnight."

"Good night, princess," Heath said, squatting in front of her.

She wrapped her arms around his neck, and he stood up, picking her up with him. Kissing his cheek, she then leaned toward me, giving me a hug and kiss, before leaning back up to him.

"You make my mom happy," she said.

"She makes me happy," he replied, turning to look at me.

"Come on, Paisley," Aunt Cindi called.

Heath put her down, and she ran over to my aunt. The rest of my family waived to me before leaving the room.

"Are you ready?" Heath asked, his voice right next to my ear as he wrapped his arms around my waist from behind.

"I am," I said.

Stepping out from behind me, he took my hand and led me from our reception.

HEATH...

The key card didn't want to work in the door, and it was more than pissing me off. I wanted this door open so I could get her inside and out of all that lace.

"Here," she said, taking the piece of plastic from me.

With an easy swipe, we got the green light, and she pushed the handle down and opened the door. When she went to walk in, I stopped her.

"What?" she asked.

Before she had a chance to protest, I scooped her up in my arms and carried her through the portal. I'd come up to the room before I headed down to the wedding and got everything ready. Well, I helped Zac and Shizuka, his wife, get everything set up. She was a whiz at decorating and had turned a simple hotel room into a romantic oasis filled with flowers, lace, LED candles, and everything a woman would want. I set her down in front of me and waited as she took in the room.

"How... When... Heath," her stuttered questions, then my name coming out in a hush, made it clear that it was the right choice. I'd definitely have to make sure I thanked them both immensely.

"You like it?" I asked her.

"It's beautiful," she said, her eyes taking in every inch of the space.

"I love you," I said in her ear.

She turned in my arms and pressed her lips to mine, mumbling the same words back to me. What started as a sweet kiss quickly turned to the passion that had been running through me all day. As much as I wanted to take my time pulling her from the dress, I damn near ripped it off her. Her hands were just as fevered on my own clothes, and in just a few moments, we were both standing naked in front of the other for the first time in a decade, or close to it.

"You're breathtaking," I said, the words coming out in a gust. "I don't know how, but you're more beautiful than the first time I saw you."

Moving to me, she wrapped her arms around my neck, pulling my lips to hers in a slow and sensuous kiss, deepening with each stroke of her tongue against mine. I slid my hands down her body until they were cupping her ass, and I picked her up, her legs wrapping around my waist, as I walked her to the bed. Without a second thought, I swept the comforter and top sheet from it, flower petals and the small candles flying as I did.

"Heath," she said as she saw the chaos.

"They're not lit," I replied. "They're battery run, so no fire danger."

"Okay," she said.

I gently placed her on the bed, then crawled up beside her. We'd had many conversations about protection, sex, and our expectations. She hadn't had any partners since she left, and I'd only had a handful, all of which were pretty much one-night stands with protection. Because I loved her and she'd asked, I went in and had testing done, ensuring there wasn't any chance of spreading something to her.

She was hesitant about whether she wanted to hold off on more kids, but knowing that I'd be there no matter what, we decided to leave it in the hands of fate or whatever else made those decisions. Obviously, even with protection, it hadn't prevented pregnancy, but we had talked long about it.

My hands moved along her curves, sliding along the planes I'd remembered from all those years ago. Her flesh pebbled with the movement, sucking in a breath as I reached the apex of her thighs.

"I'll go as slow as you want," I said, kissing her lips.

"Don't go slow," she said as I pulled back. "I need you, and I need you now. I've waited too long already."

I didn't need any further encouragement and moved my hand between her legs, sliding in her slick folds as she opened for me. Between my mouth, my hands, and her desire, I brought her to the pinnacle, over and over again, delighting in watching her fall over that cliff, my name on her lips. When I finally slid inside her, the sigh she gave told me everything I needed to know. I'd found my home again, and I'd never leave it.

NOTE FROM AUTHOR

Images and Blurbs available upon request.
I would ask that you obtain high quality headshots and cover art images directly through me, rather than taking them from either my website or Amazon, however, blurbs are readily available through both places.

ABOUT THE AUTHOR

Born and raised in the Pacific Northwest, CM Kane was fed a steady diet of sports, particularly baseball. Having this love of the game instilled in her at an early age, she found that nothing was better than getting lost in the game. Storytelling was another gift that was encouraged in her youth, and she's taking to the written word to explore a new aspect to the game she loves.

Social Media and Website Links:

Website:
https://www.authorcmkane.com

Facebook:
https://www.facebook.com/AuthorCMKane

Instagram:
https://www.instagram.com/authorcmkane/

Amazon:
https://www.amazon.com/author/cmkane

BlueSky:
https://bsky.app/profile/authorcmkane.bsky.social

ALSO BY C.M. KANE

Seattle Cascades

1. Extra Innings

2. Caught Stealing

3. Backstop

4. Power Hitter

5. Double Play

5.5. Find a Gap

6. Sweet Spot (Coming Soon)

7. 7th Inning Stretch (Coming Soon)

New Orleans Magicians

1. Choke Up

2. Caught in a Pickle

3. Brand New Ballgame (Coming Soon)

4. Fan Interference (Coming Soon)

5. Flashing the Leather (Coming Soon)

Austin Aces Hockey Club (Shared World)

Power Play

Anthologies

Unnerving: Eclipse

Street Justice (Limited Time)

Fooling Around Neon Lights & Country Nights

Stand Alone Titles

A Switch in Time